The Unwanted Puppy

The Unwanted Puppy

Holly Webb

Illustrated by Sophy Williams

stripes

For Zoe and Zach, Lucy and Georgia

www.hollywebbanimalstories.com

STRIPES PUBLISHING
An imprint of the Little Tiger Group
1 Coda Studios, 189 Munster Road,
London SW6 6AW

A paperback original
First published in Great Britain in 2018

ISBN: 978-1-84715-904-5

A CIP catalogue record for this book is available
from the British Library.

Printed and bound in the UK.

10 9 8 7 6 5 4 3 2

Chapter One

Zoe wandered along behind her dad, looking for daisies in the grass. She wanted the ones with the fat stalks and pink-tipped petals to make into a bracelet. There were just a few starting to open up, now that spring was coming.

She was gazing so closely at the grass around her feet that she was almost nose to nose with the dog before she saw it. She stopped, half crouching, staring into a curious, furry face. Zoe loved dogs and she thought she was good at recognizing what sort they were – she had a huge dog-breed poster on her wall. But she didn't know this one.

It had thick soft fur that was mostly black on its head, but with a white muzzle going into a white stripe up its forehead. There was a splash of gingery-brown on the sides of its muzzle and it had the most gorgeous ginger eyebrows. They stood out against its black fur and made it look very surprised to see her. Its ears were fluffy and long, and a bit like a spaniel's. Though it definitely wasn't a spaniel, Zoe was sure.

Even though the dog was quite big, Zoe thought it must be a puppy. It had that teddy-bear look – cuddly and fat-legged, as though it hadn't yet grown into its paws.

It was beautiful.

"Hello, sweetheart…" Zoe whispered, wondering if the puppy was a boy or a girl. She eyed the puppy sideways, trying not to stare too much into its eyes and make it scared. Her old dog Honey hadn't minded – she even quite liked being hugged, which lots of dogs didn't, but she had known Zoe forever.

The puppy leaned forwards – and licked Zoe's cheek, making her giggle. Without even thinking, she reached out and stroked one of its fluffy black ears. Then she stared at it guiltily. She loved dogs, but her mum and dad had made her promise never to stroke one without asking the owner if it was OK first. Not all dogs were as friendly as they looked so it was always best to ask. Zoe hadn't meant to break her promise, it was just that this cute puppy had licked her...

"You're beautiful," she murmured. "I wish I could make a big fuss of you! I'm sure you *are* friendly. Where's your owner, hey?"

She looked around. The puppy's lead was tied to the playground fence, so perhaps it belonged to one of the families who were playing inside. The playground was busy, though, just after school pick-up time, and Zoe wasn't sure who had brought the puppy.

"Zoe!" Her dad waved from the gate. "Come on!"

Zoe sighed and smiled at the puppy. "Bye, gorgeous! Maybe I'll see you again sometime," she added.

"Did you see that cute dog?" she asked her dad, as she ran up to him. "Look, over there by the fence."

"Wow. Very cute," her dad agreed.

"I don't know what sort of dog it is." Zoe said thoughtfully. "But I reckon it's a large breed – it was really big already and I think it's still a puppy."

"I don't know, either." Her dad looked back over his shoulder. "Do you really think it's a puppy?"

"Yes! Well … probably." Zoe sighed, and slipped her hand into her dad's, leaning her head against his arm. "I miss Honey."

"Me, too." Her dad sighed. "That dog reminds me of her a bit – I think it's the fluffy ears."

"Hers were even fluffier," Zoe said loyally. "She was the best dog ever."

Honey had died in the autumn the year before and Zoe had been devastated. Her parents had owned the gentle Golden Retriever from before Zoe was born, so she'd never known their house without her. She still woke up some mornings and forgot that Honey wouldn't be there when she went downstairs, sniffing and licking and loving her, all one giant wag.

"She was," her dad agreed. He was silent for a moment as they came through the park gate and out on to the road, just a little way down from their house. "Maybe we'll have another Golden Retriever one day," he suggested. "I bet you'd enjoy having a puppy."

Zoe looked up at him in surprise. After Honey had died, Dad had said he didn't want to think about having another dog, not yet. She tried to imagine a different Golden Retriever lying in Honey's favourite spot, next to the kitchen radiator. It was difficult – the new dog looked just like Honey.

Still… A puppy…! Zoe smiled to herself, thinking of walks with a dog again and curling up to read a book with a loving dog's nose in her lap. "Yeah … maybe…"

Scout turned to watch the girl walking away from the playground, his tail still wagging faintly. Was she going to come back? He had liked her petting his ears and fussing over him. He let out a hopeful whine, standing up to peer further around the fence. But she was gone.

The puppy heaved a sigh and slumped down, stretching out his fat tan and white forepaws and resting his muzzle on them. He wished Jack would hurry up and come and play with him. It wasn't much fun sitting here. He could hear baby Tilly wailing and he sat up again, looking worriedly into the playground. Jack was on the top of the climbing frame and Tilly was in the pushchair, with her mum leaning over to comfort her. Everything was all right…

Still, he stayed watching, ears
pricked a little. Tilly's crying made him
feel anxious, as if he ought to be doing
something to help her, but he didn't
know what. Jack was coming back
across the playground now, looking
a bit grumpy. They were about to go
home, Scout realized, wagging his
tail so hard that it thwacked against
the bars of the fence. Jack came

hurrying over to pet him and untie his lead. Scout bounced around his feet, whining and jumping excitedly, while Jack giggled. As Jack and Tilly's mum came out of the playground gate, Jack called, "Can Scout pull me?"

Scout looked round curiously as Jack picked up his scooter, which had been lying against the fence. His tail began to wag again – he knew this game! He began to pull hard against the lead. Jack squeaked and sprang on to his scooter as Scout raced down the path, Jack and the scooter bumping and rattling behind him. They bounced and clattered towards the park gates, with Jack giggling and Scout panting happily. Playing with Jack was his favourite thing to do.

Chapter Two

Zoe kicked the tennis ball towards
the fence, catching it with the side of
her foot on the rebound. She kept on
tapping and catching the ball until
at last it bounced off into a flower
bed and she had to crawl through the
bushes to find it. It was one of Honey's
old toy balls, Zoe realized, as she
picked it up. She used to throw it for

Honey to fetch all the time.

Zoe wandered back up the length of the garden with the ball in her hand. What would it be like to have another dog? Honey would have been out here with her, racing up and down, desperate to play. Even though she'd slowed down a lot in her last year, she still loved to run. Zoe had even built her an agility course out of old flowerpots and garden sticks – she'd been very good at weaving in between them. It would be a lot of fun to teach a puppy to do things like that… Zoe smiled to herself, imagining that gorgeous puppy from the park trying to fit between the sticks. From the look of it, the puppy was the perfect size now, but it wouldn't be long before it was just too huge.

She left the ball on the patio bench and hurried inside, remembering that she'd wanted to find out what sort of dog it was. She started off looking at the dog-breed poster on her bedroom wall, but she'd been right, it definitely wasn't on there. It was a bit similar to the sheepdogs, but the colouring wasn't quite the same and Zoe was sure it was bigger all over. She grabbed her book of dog breeds off the shelf instead and started to flick through. She had a feeling that maybe the puppy was some kind of shepherd dog, so she started off in the Working Dogs section, laughing at the photo of a massive black Newfoundland. It really did look like a teddy bear.

Then she turned over a couple of pages and her face lit up in a smile. "Yes! That's you!" The dog in the book was fully grown, not a puppy like the one she'd seen, but the markings were almost identical. "A Bernese mountain dog…" Zoe murmured. She'd never even heard of them before. One of the smaller photos showed two Bernese mountain dogs pulling a little cart with two toddlers sitting in it. It made it clear just how enormous the dogs were. "*These giants are gentle but determined*," Zoe read aloud to herself, leaning back against her bedroom wall and smiling. She was trying to imagine that lovely chunky puppy all grown up. It was going to be so handsome.

The next day, Zoe kept a hopeful eye out as she and her mum headed home from school through the park, looking for the Bernese mountain dog. She gave a delighted squeak as they got close enough to see the playground. Her mum glanced at her in surprise. "What is it? Have you seen one of your friends?"

"No, it's that puppy! Oh, I forgot, you didn't see it yesterday, it was Dad." Zoe's mum and dad took turns picking her up from school – it depended on who was working where. Luckily they both got to work from home some of the time. "It's a Bernese mountain dog, I think, I looked it up last night. It's so cute."

Zoe's mum peered at the dog across the park. "It looks quite big."

"If it is a Bernese, it's going to be massive. They can pull carts!" Zoe looked sideways at her mum. "I sort of accidentally stroked it… I didn't mean to! I wasn't looking and it licked me, and I patted its ears…"

Her mum rolled her eyes. "Why am I not surprised?"

Zoe giggled. "But I'd really like to see who it belongs to, so I could ask to stroke it properly. And maybe find out what it's called."

"Well, you're in luck." Her mum nodded towards the puppy. "I think that must be its owner, with the pushchair."

"Oh, yay! Hurry up, Mum." Zoe grabbed her mum's arm, and started to tow her across the park. There was a little boy standing close to the puppy now as well. He was wearing the same school uniform as Zoe. "Oh, he goes to Gardner Lane, too. I don't think I've ever talked to him, though. He looks as if he's in Reception, or Year One maybe."

As they came closer to the little

group round the puppy, Zoe slowed down a bit, feeling shy. The lady with the pushchair was strapping in a little girl and she looked up curiously as Zoe came over to her.

"Um, hi!" Zoe felt her cheeks go pink. "I just wanted to ask about your dog… Is it a Bernese mountain dog?"

The puppy's owner smiled at her. "Well done! Most people don't know what he is."

"He's called Scout!" the little boy told Zoe proudly. "He's from Switzerland."

"Sort of," his mum agreed. "Scout didn't actually come all the way from Switzerland, did he, Jack? But Bernese mountain dogs are from Switzerland."

"I saw him here yesterday and I went and looked it up," Zoe admitted. "I hadn't heard of Bernese mountain dogs before. He's beautiful."

"You can stroke him, if you like," the puppy's owner told her. "He can be a little nervous sometimes, though, so be careful. He does jump up."

Zoe nodded, moving a little closer to Scout, but not looking him straight in the eyes. It was the way Mum had explained it was best to get to know a dog – to let the dog come to her, instead of marching straight up and expecting the dog not to mind being patted or hugged.

The big puppy sniffed at her eagerly, his heavy tail waving, and then nudged his cold nose into her hand. Zoe crouched down and ran her hand gently along his back.

"You're very good with him," his owner commented, smiling at her.

"He's lovely!" Zoe told her. "Oh!" She looked on a little worriedly as Jack bounced up behind Scout and tried to stroke him, too. The puppy backed away as the little boy grabbed at his collar, his paws skittering on the tarmac.

"Careful now, Jack." His mum leaned over, murmuring gently to the dog. "It's OK, Scout. Good boy."

Jack looked at Scout and Zoe anxiously. Zoe could see Jack didn't really understand what he'd done wrong – he had just wanted to hug his big teddy-bear dog. He probably didn't realize that he was making Scout feel scared. She smiled at him. "You're so lucky to have him," she said. "He's so big and so fluffy!"

"Yes!" Jack agreed, cheering up. "He pulls me along on my scooter. He's really strong."

"We need to be getting home now," Jack's mum said. "Say goodbye, Jack." She smiled at Zoe and her mum. "Maybe we'll see you in the park tomorrow. It's nice for Jack to talk to one of the older children from school. We've only just moved here and he's having to get used to a new class. It's great having this park so close to the school, though."

Zoe nodded – so that was why she hadn't seen Scout around before. She knew almost all the dogs in the park to say hello to, as they walked through it every day on the way home from school.

"Bye! See you tomorrow!" She watched Scout and Jack and his mum heading off down the path, feeling a little envious.

"Isn't he beautiful?" she said to her mum, as they set off for the park gate.

"He really is," her mum agreed. "I'm not sure I'd be able to cope with two small children and a huge dog, though. Jack's mum must be even more of a dog fan than you."

Zoe grinned at her. "Not possible."

Over the next couple of weeks, Zoe saw Scout and his family almost every day after school, and sometimes on the way to school, too – Jack's mum, Lauren, brought him with her when she dropped Jack off. Zoe's mum and Lauren chatted to each other. Zoe's mum said she thought she was quite lonely – the family had moved because Jack's dad had got a new job and she didn't know that many people in the area yet. It was nice for Jack as well – Zoe always said hello to him at break time. She even heard some of the other boys in his class asking Jack if she was his sister. It made him look cool, knowing one of the older children.

"You can't wait to get to the park and look for that dog, can you," Zoe's dad said, laughing at her as she hurried along the pavement one afternoon. He heaved a dramatic sigh. "I wish you were that excited about seeing me…"

"Ah, Dad…" Zoe raced back and hugged him. "I do like seeing you – but—"

"I'm not a dog, I know."

"There they are!" Zoe waved to
Jack, who was on the path up ahead.
The Reception class came out ten
minutes before the rest of the school,
so Jack was usually at the park before
they got there. Jack didn't wave back,
though – he seemed to be arguing
with his mum,
and Zoe wasn't
sure he'd noticed
them coming up
behind.

"I want to go on the slide!" He glared angrily at Lauren.

Zoe hung back – she was keen to say hello to Scout, who was looking miserable, but she didn't want to make anything worse.

"I know you do," Lauren said patiently. "But Scout hasn't had a proper walk today! I was late picking up Tilly from the childminder this morning, so Scout missed his walk. We haven't got time for both, Jack, and it's not fair on Scout to make him sit outside the playground right now..."

"It's not fair on *me*!" Jack wailed. "I want to go on the slide!" Then he noticed Zoe and her dad, dawdling along the path. "She can take Scout for a walk."

"Oh…" Lauren glanced round and smiled at Zoe, and then at her dad, looking a bit embarrassed. "Sorry. No, Jack, that's silly."

"I could take him for a run about, if it helps?" Zoe put in eagerly. "I mean, if that's OK, Dad?"

Her dad nodded. "We've got time." He shrugged his shoulders at Lauren, grinning. "Zoe used to get in a real tizz if I wouldn't let her go on the swings… I know how you feel."

Lauren smiled, looking relieved. "Oh, if you really wouldn't mind, that would be such a help. We're having trouble fitting proper walks in just now. Jack's dad always used to walk Scout at lunchtime, but he can't do that with his new job. Scout knows you, so I'm sure he'd love it. Just be careful, Zoe, he *is* very strong. And don't let him off the lead, will you? He's not good at coming back. We need to do some more obedience classes, but I haven't found a session we can get to yet."

Zoe nodded. "I'll make sure I'm holding him tight. And Dad'll be there, too." She beamed at her dad as Lauren put the lead into her hand, and Scout pulled eagerly, his tail suddenly speeding up. The park was huge – she and Mum and Dad used to bring Honey here nearly every day.

"Shall we run?" she whispered to Scout. "Shall we? Would you like that?"

Scout's tail wagged even faster and

he gave a tiny woof. Zoe laughed and raced off across the grass with the puppy bounding beside her, his ears flapping and his paws thumping the grass.

It was the best feeling ever.

Chapter Three

Scout paced up and down the kitchen, whining over and over. He was worried and lonely. Everyone was out and he wasn't used to it. Usually either Lauren or her husband, Ben, was at home and he felt safe. Even if Lauren or Ben weren't paying him attention, he knew that they were there. But over the last few days, they had been going out and leaving him behind for what seemed like forever. It made him miserable. He didn't understand what was going on and he wanted his people back.

He had watched Lauren and Jack and baby Tilly leaving this morning, and realized that it was going to happen again. What if they never came back? He had started to whine, but Lauren hadn't understood that he was worried, and Jack had just told him to shh.

Scout was tired, and his basket was right there, nice and warm by the radiator, but he couldn't seem to stop pacing. Maybe he'd never see them again? He whined louder and then slumped down suddenly, lifting his nose to the ceiling in a long howl, fear and loneliness taking over for a moment. He lay on the kitchen floor, howling and howling, until there was a loud thumping against the wall and a muffled shouting. Scout didn't understand that it was the man next door, annoyed by the noise, but he could tell that the shouting was angry and it frightened him even more.

Anxiously, he slunk into the living room, away from the kitchen and the scary shouting. He tucked himself away behind the end of the sofa – it was a tight fit for such a big puppy, but he felt safer in the small space.

He was still upset, though.

Scout listened, hunched and tense in the tiny space, wondering if the angry noises were still going on. The panicked

feeling inside him was building up
again and he pawed anxiously at the
side of the sofa, scrabbling harder and
harder with his claws. Somehow, the
clawing seemed to help him feel a
little calmer, and he went
on, shredding the fabric
with his claws till it hung
down from the sofa in
tattered ribbons.
There was yellow
foamy stuff
behind the fabric
and that pulled
out, too, if he bit
at it. Scout scrabbled
and chewed and gnawed,
and some of the miserable feeling inside
him went away.

Scout heard the footsteps coming to the door, and he jumped up, full of relief and excitement. They were back! They hadn't abandoned him! He dashed to the door and leaped at it, his paws slipping and sliding on the smooth wood. He could hear Lauren laughing on the other side of the door.

"Hello! Hello, Scout! Yes, we're back. Did you miss us? I know, it's not fair, is it? I didn't have time to come and get you before I went to get Jack. Are you hungry?" She nudged Scout gently out of the way so she could get the pushchair over the front step. "No running out. Good boy. Hey, don't jump up…" Lauren pushed Tilly inside and turned to shut the door.

Scout knew he wasn't supposed to jump up at the pushchair, but he was so desperate to see them all – to love them, to show his family how much he had missed them.

"No, down," Lauren said firmly, and Scout backed off from the pushchair and turned to greet Jack instead. But the little boy stumbled away from Scout's scratchy paws as the puppy tried to jump up and lick his face.

"Mummy! He's hurting me!" The frightened tone in Jack's voice made Scout's ears flatten and he backed away. Had he done something wrong? He just wanted to be with them…

"Mummy, look!" Jack was standing in the living-room doorway, staring at

the sofa and the floor. Lauren lifted
Tilly out of the pushchair and followed
him in.

"What's the matter? Oh *no*…"

"Was it Scout?" Jack asked, and
hearing his name, Scout looked at them
worriedly. Their voices were cross.

"It must have been. It's ruined. The new sofa! Oh, you bad dog!"

Scout retreated down the tiny hallway, his head hanging and his bottom in a crouch. What had he done? He'd been so desperate to see them and now Lauren was angry. He just didn't understand.

"Hi, Zoe!"

Zoe looked round from where she was sitting chatting with her friend Lucy and waved at Jack, smiling. A group of Reception children were kicking a ball around the playground.

"Hi! Are you playing football with the others?"

"Yes – I just came to tell you about yesterday. Guess what Scout did!"

"I don't know... Um... Did he pull you to school on your scooter?"

"No! He chewed up our sofa! He really wrecked it. Mum was so cross. We came in from school and there were bits of it all over the floor. She had to put a blanket over the end of it so we could watch TV, otherwise we'd have been sitting *in* the sofa!"

"Oh no. Why did he chew it up?"

Jack shrugged. "Don't know. Mum said maybe he didn't like being left on his own when she had to go to work and Dad did, too."

Zoe nodded. "Ooops." Some dogs really hated being on their own. Honey hadn't liked it much, either, but luckily her mum and dad had managed to work their shifts round looking after Zoe and being home enough of the time that Honey didn't get too upset. And sometimes her gran had popped in to see Honey if they were going to be away for more than a couple of hours.

"Mum shut him in the kitchen today – there's not much he can chew in there, she said."

It didn't sound like much of a fun day for Scout, Zoe thought, locked up in the kitchen. She wondered if Lauren would bring him to school to pick up Jack that afternoon. She'd missed seeing him the day before because she had football club after school, but it sounded as though Lauren hadn't brought Scout on the school run anyway.

"I've got to go, it's my turn in goal! See you later, Zoe!" Jack suddenly raced away and Zoe waved after him. She watched Jack running around with his friends and bit her lip, feeling worried. Jack seemed to be really settling in, but what if Scout was getting himself into more trouble, stuck at home on his own?

Chapter Four

When Zoe came out of school, she spotted her mum waiting for her in the playground.

"See you tomorrow!" Zoe called, waving goodbye to Lucy.

"Did you have a good day?" her mum asked, giving her a hug.

"Um-hmm." Zoe nodded. "Oh, Mum, look! Scout's here!"

Her mum looked round. "What, in school? I thought dogs weren't allowed in the playground."

"No, over there by the gate." Zoe pointed to the puppy, whose lead was tied on to the railings. He was watching the children streaming out of the gate and wagging his tail at them hopefully. "He doesn't seem worried, does he?"

Her mum looked confused. "Why would he be worried?"

"I was talking to Jack at lunchtime and he said that Scout had chewed up the sofa yesterday when he was on his own. Jack said he really wrecked it. But he doesn't look as though he minds being left alone right now."

Her mum sighed. "Ugh, I remember Honey doing things like that. Once she scratched all round the carpet by the front door!"

"Did she?" Zoe blinked. She didn't remember about that.

"Yes, but you were only little. It was before we worked out we needed to get Grandma or Anna next door to pop in and see her if we were out for a long time. And I got her one of those toys that you can put treats in, that helped a bit."

Zoe nodded. "That's clever – did it stop her worrying?"

"I think so. She was distracted by the toy, you see. We put peanut butter in it sometimes, she loved that."

Lauren and Jack caught up with Zoe and her mum as they were threading their way down the path out of school, and Zoe's mum smiled. "Hello! You're out later than usual."

Lauren nodded. "Jack couldn't find his lunchbox. It took us a while to track it down."

"Are you going to the park?" Zoe asked hopefully, as Lauren undid Scout's lead. Scout nudged his nose affectionately into Zoe's hand and she smiled to herself at the chilly feel of it.

Lauren laughed. "Yes. We need to work off some of Scout's energy. He's really not liking being at home without us now that I'm working."

"Jack told me about the sofa," Zoe said, making a face.

"Our old dog Honey used to chew things when she was on her own," Zoe's mum said with a sigh. "I remember feeling as though everything had to be up on a shelf!"

"The sofa's got a big hole in it!" Jack told Zoe's mum. "Scout was so naughty."

Lauren looked suddenly tired, Zoe thought, and she felt guilty for reminding her about it. "I'm not sure what we're going to do," she said, sighing. "We love Scout, but he's quite tricky to look after, and he's growing so much! We knew how big he was going to get – we'd seen his mum. But I don't think we really understood… He's nearly the same size as Jack already."

"But he's friendly, isn't he?" Zoe asked, looking at Scout ambling along beside Jack. He really did look like a 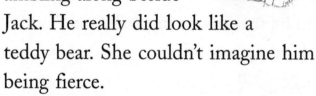 teddy bear. She couldn't imagine him being fierce.

"Absolutely! Bernese mountain dogs are really good with children, that's why we wanted to get one. It's just that Scout can easily knock Jack or Tilly over when he's excited. I hadn't realized how strong he was going to be. And he really does need a good long walk every day. It wasn't so much of a problem before – Jack's dad used to take him out. But since he's changed jobs, and I'm back at work as well…" She sighed. "I think yesterday was just too much for him. He must have been really lonely. Luckily I didn't have to do so many hours today."

"Do you have any family locally who could pop in on him while you're out?" Zoe's mum asked.

"No. All our relatives live close to our old house. We weren't planning to move, but then Ben's new job came up. We love our new house, and the new school, it's all worked out – except it hasn't worked out that well for Scout."

"Zoe, will you push me on the swings?" Jack asked hopefully, pulling her hand as they walked along the path to the little playground in the park.

"Course." Zoe grinned at him. She wanted to make a fuss over Scout, and maybe be allowed to take him for a run again, but she liked playing with Jack, too. It was like having a little brother. She followed him towards the fenced-off playground, and Jack gave the gate a push and it swung open. Zoe wondered if she should close the bolt that was supposed to stop the little ones running out, but she could see two little girls and their dad coming, so she didn't. People were always leaving the gate open.

She pushed Jack on the swings for a while, and then he jumped off and ran over to the climbing frame, clambering

up the sloping climbing wall to get
to the slide. Zoe glanced over – her
mum and Lauren were chatting by
the playground gate and it didn't look
like Mum was in a hurry to go. She
stood there half watching Jack and
half admiring Scout. He was watching
them, too, looking as though he
wished he could be with them.

"I'm good at climbing, aren't I?" Jack said to her hopefully, and Zoe turned back to smile at him.

"Really good! You got up there so fast." Zoe glanced over as she heard the gate clang again and gasped. Scout was dashing towards them, his lead bouncing on the ground. He must have pulled it out of Lauren's hand.

Zoe glanced at her mum and Lauren, and saw that they were still by the gate, looking horrified. Lauren was staring at her hand, as though she wasn't quite sure what had happened. Then she hurried towards the playground, calling, "Scout! No! Come back!"

"What's that dog doing in here?" one of the mums over by the roundabout said crossly. "Who does it belong to? No, Poppy, don't go near it!"

"He's not fierce—" Zoe started to say, as Scout came up to her, wagging his tail happily. Zoe picked up his lead and gently stroked his ears. Jack stood at the top of the climbing frame and glared at the dog. "You're not meant to be in here, Scout! Bad dog!"

Scout looked up at Zoe worriedly,

as though he thought she might tell
him off as well. The mum who'd
been standing by the roundabout was
marching towards them and Zoe
could see that Scout
was scared of her.
His ears flattened,
and he started
to lick at his nose
anxiously. "It's OK,"
she whispered.
"That dog
shouldn't be in here!"
the mum snapped at Zoe, but luckily
Lauren came over just in time.

"I'm really sorry – his lead slipped
out of my hand. Come on, Scout."
She took the lead from Zoe with a
whispered, "Thank you!" and hurried

out, ignoring the mum behind her muttering about people who didn't train their dogs properly.

Jack slid down the slide and put his hand in Zoe's. "Is she cross with us?" he asked, nodding at the other mum.

"Only a bit. Shall we go and find your mum?"

"I'm so sorry, Zoe. I hope that lady didn't upset you," Lauren said worriedly, winding Scout's lead tightly round her hand. "Scout just pulled away from me – I think he wanted to play with you and Jack."

"It was an accident." Zoe's mum patted Lauren on the arm. "Don't worry about it."

"He didn't do anything really bad." Zoe smiled at Lauren. "It's fine."

She glanced between her mum and Lauren. "I could take him for another run, like I did the other day, if you want. If it's OK with you, Mum?"

Her mum smiled at her. "I don't mind. Actually, Lauren, I was going to say, if you're ever stuck, I know Zoe would love to walk him. She hasn't stopped talking about how gorgeous Scout is since she met him. We'd quite happily exercise him for you after school if it would help. We could do most days, I think. Zoe has football after school on a Wednesday, that's all. We really miss having a dog around."

"Yes!" Zoe nodded. "It would be like we were borrowing him." She crouched down to run her hand along Scout's back and he nudged her chin lovingly.

"You really wouldn't mind?" Lauren asked. "It would be great for him to have a bit more exercise. I think it would help a lot with him being lonely at home if he was tired out!" She looked worriedly at Zoe's mum. "I don't want us to be a bother, though. It's a lot to ask. I feel like we ought to be able to look after him by ourselves."

"It would be great for us, honestly," Zoe's mum promised, and Zoe smiled at Scout, who was leaning against her heavily as she scratched his back.

"How could anyone ever think you were a bother?" she whispered in his ear.

Scout pulled a little against his lead, looking up at Zoe hopefully. He felt bouncy, full of energy, as if he could just run and run. Was Zoe going to let him race across the park with her, the way they had before? She had dashed back and forth, laughing and panting and chasing after him, and she'd never once had to stop and tie him up to a fence, or walk slowly to match the pushchair. It had just been fun.

"Shall we go for a run?" Zoe asked him, crouching down to give his ears a rub.

Scout barked. He knew that word. He skittered backwards, telling Zoe to come on, and Zoe laughed at him.

Chapter Five

"Morning, sweetie." Zoe's dad pushed the cereal box across the table towards her. Then he laughed. "I had to wake you up three times this morning and you still don't look awake."

"Nnnngh." Zoe sighed and poured herself some cornflakes. "I can't believe it's only Friday. It has to be the weekend."

Her dad shook his head sadly. "Nope. Definitely Friday, sorry. Eat up fast, Zoe, you have breakfast club today. You don't want to be late for your second breakfast!"

Zoe made a face as she poured on some milk.

"What? Don't you like breakfast club? I thought it was OK. Lucy goes, too, doesn't she?"

"Mmmm. It's just if I go to school early I don't get to watch out for Jack and Lauren bringing Scout with them." She smiled at her dad. "He keeps an eye out for me, you know? He looks all round the school playground and when he sees me his tail speeds up like a … like a ceiling fan."

Her dad nodded. "Ah… Sorry, Zoe. You really like that dog, don't you?" he added, stirring his cereal thoughtfully.

"He's the best." Zoe looked across at her dad and realized that she was stirring her bowl just like he was. "But I'm worried about him, Dad…"

"Why?"

Zoe sighed, trying to work out how to say it. "Jack really loves Scout, and so does Lauren, but he gets into trouble loads. He chewed their sofa to bits and Jack's always telling me about how he knocked something over, or chewed something else. Jack's mum's so busy with looking after Tilly and working and everything. And his dad works really long hours, so he's not home a lot." She hesitated. "It's like Scout's always the thing that comes last."

Her dad frowned. "I don't know if that's fair, Zoe. They take him for walks – we see them in the park with him nearly every day."

"Yes, but that's not a proper walk! He just gets to come along on the way to school! He needs *long* walks. He's such a big dog – and he's still only a puppy, he'll need more when he's bigger."

Her dad nodded slowly. "You really

are worried about this, aren't you?"

"Yes." Zoe heaved a massive sigh. "But we can't actually do anything about it. I mean, except help out by taking him for walks when we can. Mum said to Lauren yesterday that I could take him for a run if we see them in the park after school."

"Mmmm…" Her dad swallowed a mouthful of tea. "Those Bernese mountain dogs do need a lot of exercise. Not just walks, either. Their brains need exercise. Obedience classes, or agility."

"How do you know?" Zoe asked, very surprised. She was pretty sure her dad hadn't known what a Bernese was until she'd told him.

Her dad looked a little embarrassed. "Ummm. I might have looked them up. A couple of websites… Stop laughing at me! He's such a nice dog, I just wondered about them, that's all."

Zoe stared at her dad, feeling as though pieces in her brain were clicking into place. "You mean, maybe one day we could get one? You're thinking about it?"

"Maybe. And I haven't even mentioned it to your mum, Zoe, so you'd better not."

Zoe grinned at him.

"Finish your cereal!"

Scout peered into the hallway. He could hear people passing on the street outside – children's voices, high and squeaky, like Jack. He was sure that Lauren and Jack and Tilly would be coming home soon. It felt like way past time for a walk.

Since the day Scout had chewed the sofa to shreds, when he was home alone he had to stay in the kitchen. Lauren and Ben had bought him a special toy to keep him busy while they were gone, and he loved it. It wobbled about, bouncing over the floor as he nudged it with his nose or whopped it with a paw. He had to hit it just right to get the food out. But it was empty now, and it had been for hours, it felt like. Restlessly, Scout paced around the table again, and then again.

Then he stopped, his ears twitching eagerly. Was that voices? Footsteps outside the front door? It was hard to tell through two shut doors, but he was almost sure… Scout started to bark frantically, jumping and scrabbling at the kitchen door. It was already scarred with long scratches, the wood shredding under his claws. He could hear the front door opening now and Lauren heaving in the pushchair. Jack was laughing. Oh, how he wanted to get out of there!

"Listen to that dog! Go and let him out, Jack. I wish I'd been able to pick him up before I came to get you, but I couldn't get out of work in time."

Scout jumped and barked even louder, desperate to see his family. As Jack opened the kitchen door Scout flung himself forwards, wanting to lick them all over – to show them how much he'd missed them.

He hurled himself through the door, not realizing that Jack was standing just behind it. Scout went straight into him, his front paws right on the little boy's chest, and Jack flew backwards, landing on the hallway floor with a thump.

"Jack!"

Jack was silent for a moment, until he caught his breath, and then he howled.

Scout stared at him, horrified by the noise. He wasn't entirely sure what had happened – was Jack playing? They did roll on the floor together sometimes. He leaned over and nudged Jack's cheek with his nose.

"Bad dog! Get away!" Lauren scolded and Scout flinched. He crept along the wall to hide in the corner by the front door where the wellies were. He wasn't really sure what had happened. It had all been so quick. He'd only wanted to say hello – it had been such a long day shut in the kitchen all by himself…

Scout watched as Lauren picked Jack up, fussing over him and stroking his head anxiously. Jack was still crying and now Tilly was wailing, too. Scout pressed further into the corner, trying to make himself small enough that no one would see him and shout.

Scout finished his bowl of food, and looked over at Lauren, wondering when he was going for a walk. She'd let him into the garden for a wee, but that was all. He hadn't been out since Ben had taken him for a quick sprint along the road and back that morning before he left for work. Scout slumped down by the back door sadly, thinking of Zoe racing him across the park and laughing. He was bored – and he felt lonely, even though his people were right here. Jack was still cross with him, he could tell. He kept glaring whenever Scout looked at him.

When Ben got back, Scout bounced up to him hopefully, but all he got was a quick ear scratch, and then Jack grabbed his dad's hand and climbed up his legs for a cuddle, telling him all about his accident.

"I banged my head on the floor! I really did. It went thump. Mummy shouted at Scout!"

"Oh no, love, what happened?" Ben looked over at Lauren anxiously.

"It wasn't really Scout's fault. I think he jumped up just at the wrong time. He was so excited to see us – you know he hates being shut up on his own while we're all out." Lauren sighed. "He just ploughed Jack over. He's getting so strong…"

73

Jack's dad hugged him tighter, and made sympathetic noises about the lump on his head, and then Jack wriggled away and went back to playing with his cars.

"Do you think he's OK? He doesn't look as if it's hurting that much," Ben said, shrugging off his jacket and sitting down at the table.

"I think he's fine – this time. I was so worried, though." Lauren shook her head. "I just don't know what we're going to do, Ben…"

Ben made a face. "I know. We weren't expecting the new job and the move to happen, that's all. When we first got Scout we had plenty of time for looking after him. But now – we're not doing a very good job, are we, boy?"

Scout hurried over to him, resting his muzzle lovingly on Ben's leg. He closed his eyes blissfully as Ben pulled gently on his ears. Yes! At last someone was fussing over him, like he wanted.

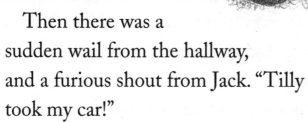

Then there was a sudden wail from the hallway, and a furious shout from Jack. "Tilly took my car!"

Ben jumped up to go and sort out the argument, gently pushing Scout away, and that was that. Everyone seemed to be busy, racing about and hardly noticing him at all.

Scout gave up and took his chew toy over to the nest he'd made among the wellies. There was a little draught coming in under the front door – a fresh scent of outdoors and the cut-grass smell of the park.

He could go by himself, Scout thought sadly, pressing his nose against the crack. He knew the way. He might even find Zoe. His tail thumped on the carpet at the thought of her. Yes! He would go to the park and find Zoe – she was always there when he was. Why shouldn't he?

It was just then that he heard footsteps hurrying up to the door and the doorbell rang. Scout jumped back in surprise at the shrill noise, his tail swishing uncertainly. He watched as Jack came racing down the hall shouting, "Nannie! Nannie!" and reached up to open the front door.

There was someone on the doorstep, but Scout hardly saw them. He only saw the path and the pavement and the swinging gate in between.

The pavement led to the park and to Zoe – someone who wanted him. He raced out of the door before anyone could stop him.

Chapter Six

Zoe sat on her bed, with her mum's laptop balanced on the pillow. All day at school she'd been thinking about her conversation with her dad – the amazing idea that perhaps they could have a Bernese mountain dog of their own!

Zoe had been hoping to meet up with Scout and Jack and Lauren in the park after school and take him for a walk – she'd thought maybe she'd also get the chance to ask Lauren about a fun agility class or something like that for Scout. It might help to wear him out and keep his brain busy. She'd been sort of looking forward to asking about it, and sort of not. She didn't want Lauren to think she was sticking her nose in…

Zoe sighed. She hadn't realized until today quite how much she looked forward to seeing Scout – she'd been so disappointed to miss him. Meeting up with him in the park was one of the highlights of her day. Zoe was almost sure that her mum and dad felt the same. She'd noticed that she and Mum both speeded up as they went in the park gates on the way home from school. They'd hurry along the paths, scanning the park to see where Scout was. Dad was just the same, always looking hopefully for the big puppy on their walk to school. Today they hadn't seen him at all – Zoe had met Jack and Lauren and Tilly hurrying through the playground, and Lauren had explained that she hadn't had time to go home and get Scout that afternoon. She'd even been a bit late picking Jack up, she said. Zoe felt as though she'd missed out on something special. She sighed again and peered thoughtfully at the list of websites on the screen. There seemed to be loads of links to pages about Bernese mountain dogs – some were the websites of breeders and some were clubs for owners. She chose one of the club pages and clicked on *Things to Know*. If Dad was really serious about them getting a Bernese one day, she wanted to be prepared.

Zoe found herself nodding thoughtfully as she read down the page. A lot of the information seemed to tie in with what she'd noticed about Scout. She'd seen him start to look worried and jumpy when Tilly was crying, and it said here that some Bernese could be sound-sensitive – that high-pitched noises almost hurt their ears.

Zoe nibbled her lip worriedly. Lauren had said Tilly was teething and crying a lot. That definitely wasn't going to help Scout settle down. There were common-sense things the website said to think about, too – a big dog was more likely to accidentally hurt a small child. Scout was big, but he was still a puppy, so he was clumsy and not really in control of his paws…

Zoe went on reading, giggling to herself at some of the funny bits. Apparently most Bernese didn't really like playing fetch, because they just didn't see the point. The owner would throw a ball, and the dog would fetch it the first couple of times and then give up, because honestly, *why*? She could easily imagine Scout dropping a ball at her feet and glaring at her, his gorgeous ginger eyebrows twitching. *Now, look. You keep dropping it, and I keep bringing it back for you. Don't do it again! Oi! I said don't do that...* It would be so funny.

Zoe looked up from the laptop, her eyes widening. Then she turned herself round on the bed, sinking her chin into her hands. She'd just realized something – something awful.

Dad was all excited about getting a puppy, but she didn't want just any Bernese mountain dog.

She wanted Scout.

Scout raced down the pavement, ignoring the shouts behind him. It was so good not to be cooped up in the house! His paws pounded on the tarmac and his ears were flapping as he bounded along. It was a chilly evening and a little bit drizzly, but he didn't mind. The dampness felt good on his fur.

He paused for a moment at the end of the road, sniffing thoughtfully. Ben usually took him out for a short walk just before bed, so he was used to the dark. Yes, the park was this way. He trotted on, eager to go racing over the grass and to find Zoe. As he saw the park gates ahead he sped up and his

tail started to wag with excitement.
He darted in, loving the scents of cut
grass and tree blossom and other dogs.
He bounced on to the wide stretch
of grass, enjoying the feel of the soft
ground and cool grass under his paws.

For a couple of minutes he just ran,
feeling the stretch in his legs as he
snapped at imaginary butterflies and
chased his own tail round and round.
Then he slumped down into a happy,
panting heap and started to wonder
where Zoe was.

He had expected to find her – or rather, he'd expected her to find *him*. She always did. He looked round eagerly, hoping to see her hurrying down the path towards him, excited and waving. But there seemed to be no one in the park at all. It was eerily quiet.

Scout sat up, and gazed around worriedly. He hadn't thought about what he might do if he couldn't find Zoe. He had just expected that she would be there. She always was...

Except, maybe this time she wasn't? His ears twitched at the strange sounds of the birds rustling in the trees and he stood up, pacing around in a tiny circle. Zoe was in the park when he was there with Jack, Scout realized. Now it was the wrong time – it was dark, closer to the time he went out for a last walk before bed.

Zoe wasn't here. He was all alone.

Tucked away under the little climbing wall that led up to the playground slide, Scout gazed out at the damp morning, wondering if he should try to find his way back home. He was sure he could do it – he'd done this walk so many times. But something was stopping him. He kept remembering Jack howling when he'd knocked him over by accident and then Lauren's sharp voice. They had both sounded so angry and upset.

Somehow his home wasn't a place

he felt happy in any more and Scout didn't really understand how that had happened.

A few times during the night the cold had woken him and Scout had wanted to go home. But the padding of strange paws past his hiding place had made him tuck his tail between his legs and wriggle further under the leaves in the corner, and he wished he'd never run away. He knew home. He was safe there, at least, and warm. A couple of times he'd got as far as the gate of the little playground before he remembered how cross everyone was and how he hated being shut up in the kitchen on his own. Each time, he'd turned back from the gate and gone to curl up by himself again.

Now Scout's tail thumped against
the dry leaves as he heard voices in the
distance. Zoe! She'd come to find him
at last! He wriggled out of his hiding
place just as a dad with two little girls
pushed open the gate. Scout's tail
drooped again as one of the little girls
raced towards the climbing wall and
then stopped dead.

"A dog!" she squeaked. Scout came
out from under the sloping wall, his
tail beating nervously from side to side.

"Hey, Olivia, come away!" the little girl's father said sharply. "Don't touch the dog. We don't know if it's friendly. It must be a stray – there's no one else here."

The little girl ran back towards her father, and he shooed her and her sister out of the way. Then he came closer to Scout, crouching low and flapping his hands. "Come on. Out!"

Scout tucked his tail down, crouching. He'd done something wrong again, he could tell. These people were angry with him, too. He scuttled forward, trying to avoid the cross-sounding man, and darted out of the gate.

Now that he was up and walking, Scout realized how hungry he was.

Perhaps he should just go home after all? But the path back to the gate led past the playground again. He didn't want to go that way and be shouted at. So he kept on, wandering along the path that led to the other side of the big park and another gate. He didn't usually come this way with Lauren and Jack and he stood uncertainly in the opening, wondering where to go and what to do.

He felt more alone than ever.

Chapter Seven

"But I thought *all* dogs liked playing
fetch? You mean they don't even
chase sticks?" Zoe's dad sounded quite
shocked, she thought. She grinned
at him, shrugging. It was so exciting
talking to him about Bernese dogs
like this. It made it seem all the more
possible that they might get another
dog of their own soon. *Even if it's not*

Scout… a little voice said in the back of her mind. Zoe squashed it down again. Scout belonged to another family. He was Jack's dog. She was going to have her *own* dog.

"That's what this website said. I suppose chasing sticks might be different… I don't know. It just said they think fetching is boring. I can see why, can't you?"

"Mmmm. It really does sound as though they're very intelligent." Zoe's dad glanced down at his watch. "We'd better walk a bit faster if we're going to get to this dance class on time, Zoe. It's almost ten!"

Zoe wasn't listening. "Dad, look!" She grabbed his arm. "Look! Isn't that Scout?"

"What? Oh, are they out for a walk?" Her dad looked up and down the street, obviously expecting to see Lauren or Ben.

"No, look, there behind that parked car. *It is!*"

Zoe stuffed her dancing bag into Dad's arms and raced up the road. She was almost sure that the black and tan and white dog peering round the car was Scout, but he was all on his own. Lauren never let him off the lead, because he wasn't reliable enough at coming back.

"Did you pull your lead out of her

hand?" Zoe asked gently, stopping a little way from Scout and the car. He looked nervous and she didn't want to scare him and make him run into the road. But he darted towards her, licking her hands and whining delightedly. "Hello! Oh, you're such a lovely dog! But where's Lauren, Scout? Where's Jack?"

"Hello, boy," her dad panted. "So it is you…" He crouched down to make a fuss over Scout, too. "Can you see Lauren or Ben, Zoe? Scout shouldn't be out on the pavement like this."

"I know," said Zoe. "I thought he must have pulled his lead out of Lauren's hand, but he hasn't even got his lead on. Just his collar. And they don't let him off the lead…"

"Ohhh… Have you gone walkabout?" Dad murmured to Scout, rubbing his ears. "Maybe he slipped out of their garden."

"What are we going to do?" Zoe asked. "We ought to take him home, but I only know they live on the other side of the park. I think they go to the gate at the bottom of the hill."

"Mmmm." Dad looked thoughtful. "We could walk down that way; we might meet them coming to look for him. But then we're not even sure if they know he's gone… Oh! Dancing!" He looked at his watch again and made a face. "Zoe, it's starting right now!"

"But taking Scout home is way more important," Zoe said indignantly. "We can text Miss Julia. She won't mind, Dad, honestly."

"Mmmm. Well, I guess you're right. We can't just leave him here. Has he got a tag on that collar?"

"Yes, and there's a phone number. We can call them."

Dad sighed. "Except I haven't got my phone with me. We'll have to take him home and do it." He unzipped Zoe's dance bag. "Do you think we could tie your ballet tights through his collar? I don't want to risk him running out into the road."

Zoe laughed. "Yes, but we'd better not tell Mum. She said those tights were really expensive."

Carefully, she looped the tights through Scout's collar and turned to lead him gently back towards their house. "Come on, Scout…" She wasn't sure if he'd want to follow her – after all, he didn't know her that well and he wasn't used to going in this direction. But he padded along beside her quite happily, every now and then looking up at her, as if to check that she was still there.

"He's walking very well," Dad said. "Not pulling at all. I was a bit worried he'd be too strong for you, but he's being very calm."

"He's gorgeous," Zoe said with a tiny sigh. She wished it was a longer walk home. As soon as they called the mobile number on his collar, Lauren or Ben would come and pick up Scout, and it was so lovely pretending that he was hers and they were just out for a weekend stroll.

She led Scout into their driveway and Dad unlocked the front door to let them in. Zoe's mum obviously heard them from the kitchen. "Was dancing cancelled?" she called.

99

"No…" Zoe called back. "We found Scout! He's run off, Mum. We've got to call Lauren to come and get him." Quickly, she whisked her dancing tights off Scout's collar and stuffed them back into the bag. Her dad winked at her.

"Oh, my goodness…" Her mum appeared in the kitchen doorway. "Hello, sweetheart! What were you doing, running about on your own? Thank goodness you two found him before he went into a road," she added.

"I know. I didn't have my phone though." Zoe's dad walked into the kitchen and picked it up from the counter. "There's a mobile number on his collar tag." He crouched down beside Scout, trying to read the tag and tap in the number while Scout licked his chin and tried to climb on top of him. "You daft dog... Oh... It's not ringing. It says that number's not in use."

Zoe's mum frowned anxiously at Scout, who'd followed Zoe into the kitchen. "Hmm... I suppose Jack's dad has just changed jobs. Maybe that was an old work phone. Now what are we going to do?"

"We could call school," Zoe suggested, almost reluctantly. She didn't really want to help find a way to give Scout back. But Jack must be so worried about him. She could imagine how she would have felt, if it were Honey.

"That's a good idea, sweetie, but I

don't think anyone's in on Saturdays."
Mum sighed. "Oh! Are you hungry,
puppy?"

Scout was sniffing hopefully at the
edge of the table. He could obviously
smell Zoe's mum's half-eaten piece of
toast.

Zoe's mum eyed it, and then the dog.
"No… I'd better not send you home
with bad habits. I bet you're not allowed
to eat from the table." She went to the
big kitchen cupboard and dug around
in the back of it. "I thought so. I tried
to throw it away a couple of times but it
made me so sad…" She held up a bag of
Honey's food.

Scout bounced and woofed excitedly
as he heard the dog biscuits rattling
in their bag, and he practically danced

when Zoe's dad found Honey's old bowl and they poured in a large helping. "After all," Zoe's mum murmured, "we don't know when he got out. He might not have had breakfast."

"He doesn't look like he did," Zoe said, giggling as Scout wolfed down the biscuits. "Here, you'd better have some water, too."

Scout finished the food and licked thoroughly round the bowl, obviously trying to make sure he hadn't missed any. Then he had a huge drink of water and sighed happily.

"He's so lovely," Zoe said, as he came to nuzzle against her knees and began to lick her fingers. "If we can't find out their number, can we keep him until school on Monday?" For a tiny moment she imagined keeping him forever – not telling Lauren and her family that they'd found him. But she knew it was only a silly daydream. "I bet they're really missing you," she murmured to Scout.

"I've just realized something!" Mum brightened up. "He must be microchipped, mustn't he? It's the law.

So all we need to do is nip down to the vet's and get them to scan him – they'll have his address on the computer."

"Oh yes." Zoe stared down at her feet. Of course, that was the sensible thing to do…

Chapter Eight

Unfortunately, the phone number on Scout's microchip was the same out-of-date one that was on his collar. The vet's had a back-up number, a landline, but although it rang, there was no answer.

"I expect that's their old house number. But I don't understand why they wouldn't have updated all the details when they moved?" Zoe's dad said to the receptionist, shaking his head.

"It happens all the time," she told him. "You'd be amazed how many people just forget to do it. I'll call back and leave a message – even if it is their old house, the new owners might have their contact details."

Zoe sat on one of the waiting-room chairs with Scout snuggled against her legs. She could tell that he didn't much like the smell of the vet's. His ears were all flattened down, and he was being very quiet and well behaved, as though he hoped no one would notice he was there. At least scanning his microchip hadn't looked as though it hurt.

"Yes, I suppose that's the best thing to do. Thanks for your help, anyway." Zoe's dad sighed and came over to Zoe and Scout. "Well, all we can do is leave a message. If they don't get back to us we really will just have to take him to school on Monday! Poor Lauren, she must be frantic, wondering where he's gone."

Zoe nodded, but she couldn't help thinking it was a little bit Lauren and Ben's own fault. They should have bought Scout a new collar tag and made sure his microchip records were up to date.

"So what do we do now?" she asked.

Her dad shrugged. "We take him home with us and wait, I suppose." He smiled at Zoe. "And make sure he's well looked after – I don't expect that's going to be a problem, is it?"

Scout stood at one end of the garden, waving his tail uncertainly. Zoe was running up and down the grass, tapping a ball between her feet. Was he allowed to join in? He'd tried to play with balls in the park before, and been told off and pulled away, but Zoe was calling to him and the ball looked so tempting…

He crept forward, nosing cautiously at the ball, and Zoe laughed. "Yes! That's it, keep going!" The ball rolled towards her and she nudged it back over to Scout. "Come on! Yes!" she squeaked excitedly as he scrabbled and pounced at the ball with his front paws and it bounced off to the side. Scout watched eagerly, settling into a hunting crouch as Zoe ran up to the ball again. This was a good game!

He chased the ball up and down the garden with Zoe until he was worn out, and then flopped down in a patch of sun on the grass. He lay there happily, panting a little. Zoe ran off into the house and Scout looked at the door, wondering if he should follow her. But then she came back out with a bowl of water for him to drink and lay down next to him. Scout drank the water greedily and then laid his nose down on his paws, sleepy in the sun. He could feel the warmth of her, lying next to his back, quiet and loving.

"Zoe!"

Zoe woke up with a jump. She hadn't

been properly asleep, just sleepy… It was so warm for springtime, and there was something so special about lying there in the sun – especially when she was curled up with a dog.

Scout sat up, too, shaking his ears and snorting a little.

"Sorry, sweetie. Were you asleep?" Dad came walking down the garden.

"Only a bit…"

"The people from Lauren's old house rang back. They had her number and I called her. I said we'd drop Scout back round – her husband's out looking for him and she's got the kids with her. Do you want to come?"

Zoe chewed her lip. She sort of didn't – but at the same time she wanted to stay with Scout for as long as possible.

"We can put Honey's old lead on him," Dad suggested. "It's still on the hook in the hall."

"Come on, Scout," Zoe called sadly, trailing back into the house. He could tell that she wasn't happy, she thought, watching him follow her, ears down. "We have to give you back," she explained as she clipped on the lead, and waited for Dad to find his keys, and Mum to grab a cardigan. "I wish we could have kept you for longer…"

The walk back to Scout's real home seemed to take no time at all, even though Zoe was trying to go as slowly as she could, and she thought Mum and Dad were, too. They stood outside Scout's house, looking doubtfully at the door, and Scout pressed himself against Zoe's legs and whined.

"I don't think he wants to go back home," Zoe said with a sniff. He didn't want to go, and she wanted to keep him. It was so unfair.

"He's probably just confused," Dad said gently and he reached out to ring the bell.

Zoe could hear footsteps and an excited voice – Jack. He must be so glad that his dog was back, Zoe told herself, trying to block out her own feelings.

"You found him for us, Zoe!" Jack squeaked, hugging her round the waist. "He ran out of the door. He was so naughty."

"It's so lucky you found him," Lauren said. "Come in – have a cup of tea. It's the least I can do to say thank you."

"Oh, that's OK…" Zoe's mum started to say, but Jack was already pulling Zoe inside and into the kitchen.

Lauren hurried around, making drinks, and Zoe watched as Scout sniffed thoughtfully at his basket and his food bowls.

"As soon as he ran off, I thought about his collar tag," Lauren explained, putting down cups of tea. "And then I realized we hadn't updated the microchip, either – I had such a long list of things to sort out after the move."

"It's a tricky time," Zoe's mum agreed. "So much to do."

Lauren sighed and looked over at Ben, who was getting biscuits out of a cupboard. "In a way this has been a good thing, though. Losing Scout 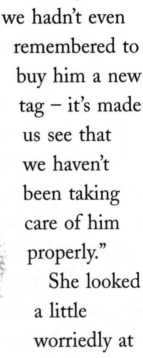and realizing that we hadn't even remembered to buy him a new tag – it's made us see that we haven't been taking care of him properly."

She looked a little worriedly at

Jack, who'd run back into the garden where he was playing with his cars. Scout was standing by the door, and watching him, but he didn't try to join in. "This morning we were talking about ringing up his breeder and getting her to take him back. We've realized we just can't cope with him and it's only going to get worse as he gets bigger. We did try to talk to Jack about it, but I'm not sure he really understands."

Zoe's mum and dad both nodded, and Zoe could hear her dad saying something about that being a sensible decision, but it was as though she was hearing him from a long way away. There was a strange sort of rushing noise in her ears, like she could hear her own heart beating. They were sending Scout back? She wouldn't even be able to see him in the park?

She wouldn't see him at all.

Her parents and Lauren and Ben went on chatting, but Zoe sat silently, not even sipping the juice that Ben had poured for her. She was almost sure that if she moved at all, she would burst into tears. She couldn't look at Scout.

It seemed hours until Mum said that they ought to make a move. Zoe stood up carefully, the way she did if she had a headache and sudden movements would hurt. It was all so wrong! When were they going to get rid of Scout? She hadn't even asked. She wasn't sure she could bear to know – but what if this was the last time she ever saw him?

Scout followed them down the hallway and Ben held on tightly to his collar as Lauren opened the front door, so he couldn't slip out again. Zoe shoved her hands into the pockets of her jeans, in case she tried to push Ben's hand away and grab Scout's collar herself. The puppy was staring at her. His tail was tucked down and his eyes looked so sad. He was unhappy, and he was going to be really confused when Lauren and Ben sent him back. Zoe's own eyes filled with tears and she turned away.

No one said very much as they walked along the street. Zoe was concentrating on not letting her mum and dad see that she was crying. They'd think she was so stupid – it wasn't as if Scout had ever been her dog. She knew that. He was just a friend, that's all.

"Zoe, which would you like?" her mum said and Zoe realized that she must have been asked a question.

"Wh-what?" she asked in a wavery sort of voice.

"Would you like mashed potatoes or— Zoe, what's the matter?" Her mum stopped and looked properly into her eyes. "Sweetheart, what is it?"

Her dad put his arm round her shoulders. "Oh, Zoe, don't cry!"

"They're giving Scout back!" Zoe
wailed. She just couldn't hold it in
any longer. "We won't even see him
now."

"We did say we'd think about getting
our own dog soon," Mum said gently.
"Maybe even a Bernese mountain dog
like Scout."

"I don't want another dog!" Zoe
looked up at her. "It won't be the

same, don't you see?"

There was a moment of strange, waiting silence, and Zoe looked up to see her mum and dad exchanging a thoughtful glance.

"You know," her dad murmured, "when they said they were going to give up Scout, I did wonder…"

Zoe's mum shook her head. "So did I! But it just seemed a bit odd to suggest we could take him!"

"You mean it?" Zoe whispered.

Her mum laughed and looked at her dad. "Yes!"

Zoe stared at them for a second more, and then she turned and raced back down the road.

Zoe held up the treat – it was a bit of cheese. She'd discovered this was Scout's favourite after he'd eaten her packed-lunch sandwiches. Scout was sitting, just about – he kept half getting up and then sitting down again because he wanted the cheese – at the end of the line of wellies Zoe had made.

"In and out! In and out, Scout!" Zoe said hopefully, crossing her fingers. Scout eyed the cheese, and then the wellies, and then marched straight down the side of the line instead of zigzagging through them like he was supposed to. Then he sat down in front of Zoe, sitting beautifully, like the best-behaved dog ever. He stared up at her with huge, dark, hungry eyes and she gave him the cheese anyway. She couldn't resist those eyes and, after all, he *was* sitting.

"How's he doing?" her mum called from the kitchen. "Have you run out of cheese yet?"

"He almost did it," Zoe called back. "And, um, yes. Can we have some more cheese, please?"

Scout turned to look hopefully towards the kitchen, too. He might not get this in and out thing, but he knew exactly what cheese was. He loved it almost as much as he loved Zoe.

Out Now

A Kitten
Called Tiger

From best-selling author
HOLLY WEBB
Illustrated by Sophy Williams

Out Now

Monty the Sad Puppy

From best-selling author
HOLLY WEBB

Illustrated by Sophy Williams

HOLLY WEBB

Holly Webb started out as a children's book editor and wrote her first series for the publisher she worked for. She has been writing ever since, with over one hundred books to her name. Holly lives in Berkshire, with her husband and three young sons. Holly's pet cats are always nosying around when she is trying to type on her laptop.

For more information
about Holly Webb visit:

www.holly-webb.com

CHASE

JAMES PATTERSON is one of the best-known and biggest-selling writers of all time. His books have sold in excess of 325 million copies worldwide and he has been the most borrowed author in UK libraries for the past nine years in a row. He is the author of some of the most popular series of the past two decades – the Alex Cross, Women's Murder Club, Detective Michael Bennett and Private novels – and he has written many other number one bestsellers including romance novels and stand-alone thrillers.

James is passionate about encouraging children to read. Inspired by his own son who was a reluctant reader, he also writes a range of books for young readers including the Middle School, I Funny, Treasure Hunters, House of Robots, Confessions and Maximum Ride series. James is the proud sponsor of the World Book Day Award and has donated millions to various independent bookshops. He lives

BOOK**SHOTS**

STORIES AT THE SPEED OF LIFE

What you are holding in your hands right now is no ordinary book, it's a BookShot.

BookShots are page-turning stories by James Patterson and other writers that can be read in one sitting.

Each and every one is fast-paced, 100% story-driven; a shot of pure entertainment guaranteed to satisfy.

Available as new, compact paperbacks, ebooks and audio, everywhere books are sold.

BookShots – the ultimate form of storytelling. From the ultimate storyteller.